What's the Weather Like?

It's Snowing

Celeste Bishop

illustrated by
Maria José Da Luz

PowerKiDS
press.

New York

Published in 2017 by The Rosen Publishing Group, Inc.
29 East 21st Street, New York, NY 10010

First Edition

Managing Editor: Nathalie Beullens-Maoui
Editor: Katie Kawa
Book Design: Michael Flynn
Illustrator: Maria José Da Luz

Cataloging-in-Publication Data

Names: Bishop, Celeste.
Title: It's snowing / Celeste Bishop.
Description: New York : Powerkids Press, 2016. | Series: What's the weather like? | Includes index.
Identifiers: ISBN 9781499423556 (pbk.) | ISBN 9781499423570 (library bound) | ISBN 9781499423563 (6 pack)
Subjects: LCSH: Snow–Juvenile literature. | Weather–Juvenile literature.
Classification: LCC QC926.37 B57 2016 | DDC 551.57'84–dc23

Manufactured in the United States of America

CPSIA Compliance Information: Batch #BS16PK: For Further Information contact Rosen Publishing, New York, New York at 1-800-237-9932

Contents

Big, white flakes are falling from the sky. It's snowing!

Snow is a kind of weather.

Snow comes from clouds in the sky.

Snow is a sign winter is here.

It snows a lot where my family lives.

9

Snowflakes can be big or small.
Each one is different.

10

I catch them on my tongue!

My mom says I can go play in the snow.

It's time to get bundled up.

I put on my boots and coat.

Gloves keep my hands warm.

15

My sister and I build a snowman.
He wears a hat and a scarf.

Poof! Something hits my coat.

It's time for a snowball fight!

My friends are sledding down a hill.

My sled goes really fast.

21

I'm cold when I get home.

Drinking hot chocolate will
warm me up. Yum!

Words to Know

boots

scarf

snowflake

Index

24